Carl's Sleepy Afternoon

Alexandra Day

Farrar Straus Giroux

New York

Many kind and cooperative people and dogs gave me their time and let me use them and their businesses in this book. My heartfelt thanks to Phyllis Jansen Eggler, Graham Palmer, Myles Andersson and their mothers; Christina Darling; Jason and Lillian Meyer; Nancy, Ford, and Winston Smith; Jack Stowe; Harold Darling; Zubiaga, Zeppo, Hazel, and Melba Toast; Epiphany School Class of 2005; Tracy Peterson and the North Hill Bakery; Lisa Plumlee and Pharmaca; Dr. Jacqueline Obando and MercyVet; Fran Carlson's Daycare; Alex Soto and Flowers on 15th; Lola McKee and Madison Park Hardware; Duane Andersen and the Seattle Fire Station No. 6; and Kate Etherington and The Children's Shop.

"We're going to do some errands and get Madeleine a new dress for Aunt Anne's wedding, so you can have a nice nap this afternoon, Carl."

"It's just me, Carl. Do you want to give me a hand?"

"Hello, Carl. You're just the one I need."

"Dr. Obando needs this right away, and the delivery boy's out."

"If that's the pharmacy delivery, bring it in here, please."

"Oh, it's you, Carl.
Good. Could you help
me for a few minutes?"

"Thanks so much, Carl.
Be sure and have a biscuit
on your way out."

"Hello, Carl. This is
my grandson, Graham."

"Let's go watch the magician, Carl."

"Ladies and gentlemen, this is Harvey. Harvey wants to see his wife, and we're going to find her for him.

"I'll put the magic box over his head and . . .

SHA-ZAM

"Presto! Here's Harvey and his wife, Daisy . . .
and . . . er . . . a surprise!"

"Let's buy some flowers, Madeleine.
Which ones do you like?"

"Come on, Carl. Mrs. Murphy's got a fire in her garage."

"Oh, do something! Matilda's in there with her babies!"

"No, Carl, that's too dangerous!"

"You're a hero, Carl!
I'm so grateful!"

"Why are you wiggling so much, Madeleine?"

"I really appreciate your patience, Kate. I don't know why Madeleine was such a jumping jack today."

"It's time we started for home, Madeleine.
Here, you can carry your new dress."